**It's the coolest school in space!**

Young Teggs Stegosaur is a pupil at **Astrosaurs ACADEMY** – where amazing adventures and far-out fun are always close by! He and his two best friends Blink and Dutch have trained hard and played hard . . . and now they've finally done it. Very soon they will be space-exploring **Astrosaurs**!

For lots of astro-fun visit the website www.**astrosaursacademy**.co.uk

D0111454

*Read the full set of Astrosaurs Academy adventures!*

*And you can follow Teggs once he's graduated as a real space-exploring astrosaur in the Astrosaurs series!*

Find out more at www.**astrosaurs**.co.uk

# Astrosaurs ACADEMY

## STEVE COLE

# Space Kidnap!

*Illustrated by* Woody Fox

**RED FOX**

SPACE KIDNAP!
A RED FOX BOOK 978 1 862 30888 6

First published in Great Britain by Red Fox,
an imprint of Random House Children's Books
A Random House Group Company

This edition published 2011

1 3 5 7 9 10 8 6 4 2

The Random House Group Limited supports the Forest Stewardship
Council (FSC), the leading international forest certification organization.
All our titles that are printed on Greenpeace-approved FSC-certified paper
carry the FSC logo. Our paper procurement policy can be found at
www.randomhouse.co.uk/environment.

**Mixed Sources**
Product group from well-managed
forests and other controlled sources
www.fsc.org   Cert no. TT-COC-002139
© 1996 Forest Stewardship Council

Typeset in Bembo MT Schoolbook 16/20pt
by Falcon Oast Graphic Art Ltd.

Red Fox Books are published by Random House Children's Books,
61–63 Uxbridge Road, London W5 5SA

www.**kids**at**randomhouse**.co.uk
www.**totallyrandombooks**.co.uk

Addresses for companies within The Random House Group Limited can
be found at: www.randomhouse.co.uk/offices.htm

THE RANDOM HOUSE GROUP Limited Reg. No. 954009

A CIP catalogue record for this book is available from the British Library.

Printed and bound in Great Britain by CPI Bookmarque, Croydon, CR0 4TD

*For David Simkins*

# WELCOME TO THE COOLEST SCHOOL IN SPACE . . .

Most people think that dinosaurs are extinct. Most people believe that these weird and wondrous reptiles were wiped out when a massive space rock smashed into the Earth, 65 million years ago.

Ha! What do they know? The dinosaurs were way cleverer than anyone thought . . .

This is what really happened: they saw that big lump of space rock coming, and when it became clear that dino-life could not survive such a terrible crash, they all took off in huge, dung-powered spaceships before it hit.

The dinosaurs set their sights on the stars and left the Earth, never to return . . .

Now, 65 million years later, both plant-eaters and meat-eaters have built massive empires in a part of space  called the Jurassic Quadrant. But the carnivores are never happy unless they're causing trouble. That's why the Dinosaur Space Service needs herbivore heroes to defend the Vegetarian Sector. Such heroes have a special name. They are called ASTROSAURS.

But you can't change from a dinosaur to an astrosaur overnight. It takes years of training on the special planet of Astro

Prime in a very special place ... the Astrosaurs Academy! It's a sensational space school where manic missions and incredible adventures are the only subjects! The

academy's doors are always open, but only to the bravest, boldest dinosaurs ...

And to YOU!

*NOTE: One of the most famous astrosaurs of all is Captain Teggs Stegosaur. This staggering stegosaurus is the star of many stories ... But before he became a spaceship captain, he was a cadet at Astrosaurs Academy. These are the adventures of the young Teggs and his friends – adventures that made him the dinosaur he is today!*

# Talking Dinosaur!

How to say the prehistoric names in
SPACE KIDNAP!

DIPLODOCUS – *di-PLOH-de-kus*

STEGOSAURUS – *STEG-oh-SORE-us*

DICERATOPS – *dye-SERRA-tops*

ANKYLOSAUR – *an-KILE-oh-SORE*

DRYOSAURUS – *DRY-oh-SORE-us*

TRICERATOPS – *try-SERRA-tops*

BAROSAURUS – *bar-oh-SORE-us*

LAMBEOSAUR – *LAM-be-uh-SORE*

CARNOTAUR – *kar-noh-TOR*

RAPTOR – *RAP-tor*

# The cadets

## THE DARING DINOS

Teggs     Dutch     Blink

## DAMONA'S DARLINGS

Damona     Netta     Splatt

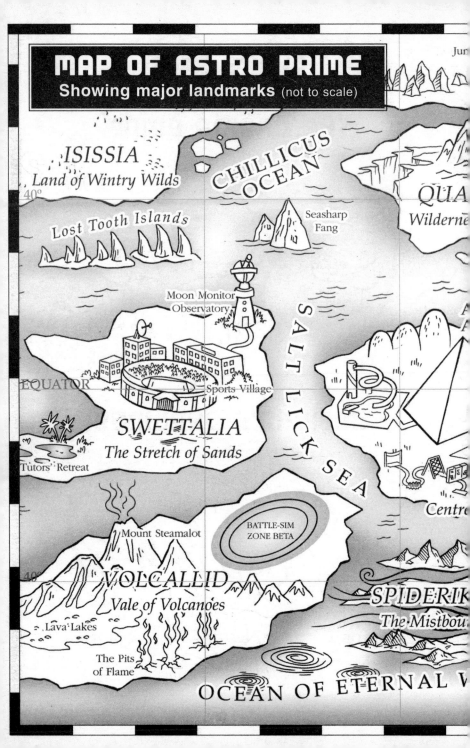

## Chapter One

# ATTACK OF THE DEATH SHIPS

Teggs Stegosaur stared at his spacecraft's
scanner screen and knew he was in a
king-sized scrape. "Raptor death ships!"
he groaned, sweat trickling down his
scaly orange-brown skin. "Six of them!"

"They've got us totally surrounded,"
said his friend
Dutch, a stocky
green diplodocus.
"And each one
has enough
firepower
to blast
us out of
the cosmos!"

Teggs turned to the yellow dino-bird beside him. "Blink — can we outrun those death ships?"

"I'm afraid not," chirped Blink, ruffling his wings as he checked the space radar. "All weapons are primed."

"Then we'll have to stay and fight," Teggs declared. "We're the Daring Dinos — so do we dare to take on these raptors?"

Blink and Dutch joined in as he yelled their team battle cry: "WE DARE!"

"OK, guys," Teggs went on. "Stand by to launch our dung torpedoes."

"Too late," cried Dutch. "The raptors are firing lasers!"

Ka-*ZUMMMMM!* The spacecraft rocked, as deadly explosions went off all around. The lights turned from white to red and a warning siren howled.

"Damage report, Blink!" Teggs shouted when the tremors had died down.

Blink peered at a screen. "Oh, no – our torpedo tubes are wrecked. We can't fire back at the death ships!"

"Not fair," cried Dutch. "We've got fifty dung torpedoes on board and we can't let off a single one!"

"Or maybe we can . . ." Suddenly, Teggs smiled. "Can we open the torpedo loading hatch?"

Blink blinked. "If we do that, the torpedoes will just fall out into space. That's not the same as firing them."

"Depends *when* we do it!" Teggs reared

up in the control pit, the bony plates on his back flushing red with excitement. "Let's fly away from them. Maximum speed."

Dutch hit the thrusters. "I'll switch on the rear scanner so we can still see them." Blink gulped at the sight of six death ships bearing down on them. "Here they come!"

"Open the loading hatch, Blink," Teggs cried. "NOW!"

Blink jabbed the button with his beak and sent a flurry of dung torpedoes tumbling out into space – straight into the path of the first speeding death ship. *BOOM! WHOOM! Ker-SQUELCH!* Dozens of disgusting explosions went off in blinding brown bursts and the death ship spun out of control – smashing into the other raptor vessels and showering them in searing dung-dollops too.

Teggs beamed at his friends. "NOW we can outrun them!"

"Wa-hooooooo!" whooped Dutch, and Blink turned a happy somersault.

"This is Astrosaurs Academy ground control to the Daring Dinos." All at once, the image of a green, long-necked dinosaur appeared on the scanner screen; he was chomping on an unripe banana like it was a cigar. "Good work, troops," he said. "The space-battle test is over."

"Commander Gruff!" Teggs quickly saluted. He was a young stegosaurus, and like his friends he wore the dark blue uniform of the coolest school in space – the Astrosaurs Academy. It was here that brave dinosaurs trained to become even braver space-dinosaurs! Commander Gruff was the head teacher and his lessons were often full-on missions, packed with danger and excitement . . .

*But this was our most important mission of all*, thought Teggs.

"That was amazing," Blink cried. "Everything seemed so real!"

"The death ships were only replicas flown by our instructors." The commander grinned. "But those were

6

real lasers they zapped you with."

"Did we pass?" Dutch asked.

Gruff nodded. "You won through in the most ingenious way I have ever seen."

"We did it." Teggs smiled at his friends with relief. "And this was our last exam!"

Blink blinked rapidly. "Tomorrow all our test results will be added together to give our final astro-score."

"If we score less than sixty, we can't be astrosaurs." Dutch shivered. "The thought of that is way scarier than raptors!"

"Perhaps this was your final exam, troops . . . and perhaps it wasn't," said Gruff mysteriously. "Now, I'd better send some mechanics to fix up those ships you clobbered. Well done again — and get your scaly butts back to the Academy. ON THE DOUBLE!"

## Chapter Two

## PASS OR FAIL?

Teggs couldn't sleep that night. He was buzzing with nerves. How have I done in my exams? he wondered. Would he soon be swapping the blue costume of a cadet for the smart red uniform of a real astrosaur?

Blink and Dutch couldn't sleep either, tossing and turning in their beds for hour after hour.

"This is crazy, guys," Teggs announced as five o'clock in the morning crawled by. "We might as well go down to the Central Pyramid and wait for our scores there."

Five minutes later, the Daring Dinos did exactly that – but Teggs soon saw that they were not the first to arrive. A red diceratops with a pretty, two-horned face was

RESULTS COMING SOON...

preening herself beneath the huge screen where the results would soon appear.

"What a surprise." Teggs eyed his biggest rival with a grudging smile. "Damona Furst! You're here early."

9

"You know me, boys – I've always been ahead of my time!" Damona stuck her nose in the air. "Besides, I just couldn't wait to find out how much I've beaten you all by!"

Blink rolled his eyes. "Where are your team-mates – still in bed?"

"As if!" A pink ankylosaur with a blue ribbon tied about her tail stomped round the corner. "I'm just too nervous to stand still so I'm pacing up and down."

Dutch smiled. "Me too, Netta. I think I'll join you!"

As Dutch and Netta strode away, Teggs looked about for the third of Damona's Darlings. "Where's Splatt?"

"In the toilet," Damona revealed. "He's really, *really* nervous!"

Splatt was a super-swift dryosaurus — but he came shuffling out of the loo at a snail's pace. "I wasn't expecting our tests to be so hard," he admitted.

"Claws crossed, we'll all have passed," said Teggs.

The hours edged by. More and more anxious cadets turned up. Dutch and Netta wore holes in the carpet with all their pacing, while Blink turned fluttery somersaults and Splatt got through thirteen toilet rolls! Teggs and Damona sat in silence, their tummies churning.

Finally, Colonel Erick, the Academy's flying instructor, breezed along the corridor. The crowd of cadets fell quiet and saluted as he approached.

"Our computers have worked out your final scores," Erick announced, pushing a computer disk into a slot beneath the screen. "Good luck, cadets – here we go!"

The screen flickered into life. Teggs held his breath as a long list of numbers and names appeared.

The name at the very top was no surprise – DAMONA FURST, 90/100.

"Yessssss!" Damona bounced around in a blue and red blur. "I won! I came first!"

With a shock, Teggs saw that his own name was second on the list – also with a score of 90.

"You came *joint* first, Damona," Blink corrected her. "With Teggs," he added proudly.

"And look!" Dutch stretched his neck and pointed with his nose. "Blink scored eighty-one, and I got seventy-six."

"That makes the Daring Dinos the number-one team!" Teggs cheered. "Woo-hoooo! We're all going to be astrosaurs!"

As Blink and Dutch piled in for a happy hug, Teggs was pleased to see that lots of his other friends had passed too.

The Baggy Brothers were dancing for joy with Trebor the triceratops. The Leaf-Loving Squad burst into a victory song.

But then Teggs noticed Netta comforting Splatt. Checking the board, he saw that Netta had got 76 out of 100, just like Dutch. But Splatt had only scored 59.

"I've failed by one point!" Splatt sobbed. "If only I'd worked harder!"

"Attention, cadets," called Erick, and everyone fell silent. "I know some of you will be very sad you haven't passed. But you don't have to go home. If you stay on and train hard for another year, you can retake your exams."

"A whole year?" Splatt sighed. "Not fair!"

"Now, there will be a party later on for

everyone," Erick continued. "Meanwhile, all cadets who scored seventy-five points or over, make your way to the main hall . . ."

Low murmurings broke the hush as the cadets with the highest marks moved off as instructed. Damona hugged the sullen Splatt and Netta kissed his cheek. Then, with sad smiles, they trooped after the other top scorers.

"That silly Splatt," said Damona. "His low score stopped us from making top team."

"I do feel sorry for him though," Netta sighed. "Doing stuff without him won't be the same."

"True — it'll be better." Dutch dodged a swipe from Damona's tail. "Just kidding! I'm sorry for the little dude."

"And everyone else who didn't make it," Teggs agreed.

"They'll be OK," said Blink positively. "They're bound to pass next time."

The five cadets went into the main hall and took their seats – just as Commander Gruff lumbered onto the stage.

"Well done, troops!" Gruff beamed around at the twenty-four dinosaurs in the room. "Without further ado, I'd like to present a very important guest – the head of the Dinosaur Space Service himself, Admiral Rosso!"

Teggs led a huge round of gasps as a crusty green barosaurus entered the hall.

"Admiral Rosso!" Blink squealed. "He's fought in more than a hundred battles!"

"He's the biggest hero in the universe," Teggs added.

Dutch started clapping, and everyone else joined in.

"Thank you!" Rosso smiled and held up a huge foot for silence. "You cadets are the best of the best. When you graduate in two days' time, you are guaranteed a place in the DSS as junior

officers. But because you have all done *so* well, I have decided to set you a special challenge – one final test."

"So *that's* what Gruff was talking about yesterday," Blink whispered.

"Imagine if I was kidnapped by enemy carnivore agents," Rosso went on. "What would happen?"

"It would be a disaster!" cried Damona.

Trebor nodded solemnly. "If the DSS

lost its leader, vital plant-eater defence secrets could fall into the wrong hands."

"Precisely," said Rosso. "Well, tomorrow – just as a training exercise, of course – I *will* be kidnapped and taken into space! Your mission will be to track me down, overcome all dangers and 'rescue' me as quickly as possible."

Teggs felt his heart pound faster in anticipation. What a mission!

"Please, sir," said Damona. "What will the winner get?"

Rosso smiled. "The cadet who shows the most courage, skill and determination will be awarded one of the most prized medals in the DSS – the Order of the Star Lizard."

The cadets clapped and jumped up and down on their chairs.

"Only five have ever been given!" squawked Blink.

18

Netta almost swooned. "Just imagine graduating from the Academy with that medal on display!"

"Settle down, troops!" boomed Gruff, marching back onto the stage. "Now, Admiral Rosso's 'kidnap' will happen in the night – and the test will begin at dawn tomorrow, here in the hall. Until then, have fun – you've earned it."

Rosso walked off with Gruff, to another round of applause, and then the cadets made their way outside.

"I wish Splatt could come on this mission with us," said Damona. "He'd love it."

"Let's check he's OK," said Netta. "He's probably sulking in his room."

Teggs watched as the girls hurried off. But then Blink pointed in the opposite direction. "Look – *there's* Splatt, over by the canteen."

"I'll just tell him his team-mates are looking for him," Teggs said. As he jogged

over, he saw that Splatt was talking to
two blue dino cleaners with a trolley
full of towels. One was short and one
was tall with a long neck. Teggs had
never seen them before. They saw him
approach, shook Splatt's hand, and then
turned and scurried away.

"Hi, Splatt," said Teggs. "Damona and

Netta are looking for you in the dino-
dorms. Are you all right?"

Splatt grinned at Teggs. "I *wasn't* all
right – but I think
I'm going to be.
Just you wait
and see."
And, with
a cheeky
wink, he
strutted off.

"By the way,
what did those
cleaners want?" Teggs called. "I didn't
recognize them."

But Splatt did not reply . . .

# Chapter Three

## THE MISSION BEGINS

The Results Day party went on late into the night. The cadets filled the canteen, dancing and eating till they were worn out and fit to burst. Everyone was there to share a fun-packed night, whether they had passed or not.

Everyone except Splatt.

"I wonder where he is?" Damona said as midnight chimed over the hubbub of happy voices. "He seemed so cheerful this afternoon, I was sure he'd come."

"Me too," said Netta, watching Dutch beat his tenth opponent in a pudding-eating contest.

"Maybe he was just putting on a brave

face," said Blink, washing down a bug sandwich with some swamp juice. "I expect he's really sad."

Teggs nodded thoughtfully. "I'll go and look for him."

"Tell him to shift his scaly butt down here," said Dutch through a mouthful of pie. "I've almost reached my one hundredth pudding!"

Teggs went out into the cool of the moonlit night and headed for the dino-dorms. He knocked on Splatt's door but there was no answer.

"Can I help you?" came a familiar voice behind him.

Teggs whirled round to find Splatt standing in the corridor – out of breath and soaking wet. "No one had seen you for ages," said Teggs. "We were worried, and so—"

"I'm fine," said Splatt. "OK?"

Teggs watched the puddle of water at Splatt's feet grow larger. "I didn't

think it was raining outside."

Splatt looked shifty. "There was,
um . . . a big downpour a couple of
minutes ago. Go back to the party now.
I'll be over when I've dried off."

"OK. See you soon." Teggs shrugged
and went outside again. The grass was
bone-dry underfoot.

"Splatt was lying to me," he muttered.
"But why?"

At daybreak the next morning, yawning
and stretching, Teggs, Blink and Dutch

made their way to the main hall – ready to rescue Rosso! But as they reached the big results screen on the way to the hall, the Daring Dinos got a surprise.

COMPUTER ERROR!

CORRECTED RESULT:

LINFORD SPLATT-
84/100

COMPUTER ERROR! The words flashed in big capital letters. CORRECTED RESULT: LINFORD SPLATT – 84/100.

"Huh?" Dutch stared. "Whaddya know – the scrawny little dude scored way better than he thought."

"He scored more than me and you, Dutch," Blink noted.

Teggs frowned, remembering Splatt's words after talking to the two cleaners. *I* wasn't *all right – but I think I'm going to be. Just you wait and see . . .*

Blink led the way into the hall, where the other cadets had already gathered. Netta and Damona were dancing about with Splatt.

"Isn't it great?" gushed Netta. "Splatt is going to be an astrosaur like the rest of us!"

"And since his *real* score is so high, Damona's Darlings are now the top team," said Damona smugly. "Not you three!"

"Congratulations," said Teggs generously. "But you don't look very surprised, Splatt. It's almost as if you knew this would happen."

Splatt scowled and seemed set to protest – when Commander Gruff came into the hall, chomping on his green banana.

"All right, troops," he growled. "You know the set-up for this special final challenge – we're pretending that Admiral Rosso has been kidnapped from Astro Prime and is being held somewhere in space. Whoever overcomes all obstacles and finds him first will win the prize." The commander paused. "And don't come bugging me for clues, because not even I know where he's hiding. No one does, except for the training robots who took him. He wanted the test to be as realistic as possible, and so until you find him, he really *is* lost in space." Gruff saluted the cadets with his front leg. "Good luck, troops." He frowned at Splatt as if noticing him for the first time. "Good luck to you all."

An excited buzz ran around the hall as the commander lumbered away. Half the cadets – including Trebor and the Baggy Brothers – dashed out at once.

"They'll be heading for the Academy's space radar tracking station, looking for any new objects in the area in case Rosso's there," Blink twittered. "We should get after them."

Teggs shook his head. "We should do something different."

Dutch nodded. "Especially if the Academy's computers are playing up. They already scrambled Splatt's score – they might mess up again."

"Hey!" Blink started blinking extra fast. "What about that brand-new astro-jet we saw in the hangar last week?"

"Colonel Erick's Mark Eight Dungbuster!" A slow smile spread over Teggs's face. "A ship like that will have a super-cool radar."

"What are we waiting for?" said Dutch eagerly. "Let's get down to—"

"THE ASTRO-JET HANGAR!" chorused Damona's Darlings.

"Oh no," said Blink. "They've had the same idea!"

Splatt took off like a streak of green light. "Go, Splatt, go!" cheered Damona.

"After him, Blink!" Teggs urged the dino-bird.

Blink shot off in hot pursuit. Teggs,
Dutch, Netta and Damona charged
down the deserted corridors at full pelt
after their friends.

"We had the idea first," Damona
panted. "You're copying."

"No way!" Dutch shot back.

Teggs saved his breath for running,
sprinting ahead as they neared the
hangar – which looked like a huge
concrete box. Blink and Splatt were
banging on some super-sized steel doors
set into the side.

"We can't get in!" Splatt complained.
Dutch looked at Teggs as Blink flew
over to join them. "It's Colonel Erick's
astro-jet – he
must have the
key to those
doors."

"I'll try to
find him,"
Blink offered,
launching
himself into
the air.

33

Damona pushed past Teggs and Dutch and squared up to the huge metal door. "If Rosso really *had* been kidnapped, a true astrosaur wouldn't let anything stand in her way." *WHAM!* She thwacked her tail against the solid steel. "Help me, Netta!"

Teggs frowned as the two girls pounded and dented the thick metal with powerful blows, desperate to get in. Even Splatt started kicking it as hard as he could. The hangar shook, and large cracks appeared in the concrete over the doors.

"Careful, dudes!"
Dutch yelled, trying
to make himself
heard over the
pounding attack.

"You're
weakening
the whole
building!"
warned Teggs.
But even as he
spoke, a massive
chunk of stone
broke away from
the high wall
and came crashing
down towards the
dinosaurs below . . .

## Chapter Four

## A BAD BREAK

Ignoring the danger, Teggs dived towards
Damona, Netta and Splatt. "LOOK
OUT!" With a staggering sweep of
his spiky tail, he pushed them clear.
But as he tried to jump after them, a
lump of concrete smashed down on his
back and slammed him to the ground.
"OWWWWW!"

"Teggs!" yelled Dutch helplessly – as plummeting brickwork struck the spot where Damona and her friends had been standing.

Splatt stared in shock. "Teggs – you saved our lives!"

"Thank you," said Damona softly, and Netta nodded her agreement.

Dutch ran to his team-mate's side. "Dude, are you OK? You took a bad hit to your backplates."

"They're OK," said Teggs. "But I landed badly. I can't move my right front leg." He saw that it had swollen up like a balloon, and his orange-brown scales were already bruising black. "One of my back legs hurts too. How can I hope to complete Rosso's special mission now?"

"You were so brave, Teggs." Splatt swallowed hard. "I . . . I'll never be like you."

"Your true test score was really high," Teggs reminded him. "You'll make a great astrosaur."

"I won't." Splatt shook his head. "I don't deserve to." Suddenly, he turned and ran away from the hangar.

"Splatt?" Damona yelled after him. "What about the challenge?"

"Go without me!" Splatt called back. "Just go!"

"What was *that* about?" Dutch wondered. Damona and Netta looked at each other, baffled.

Seconds later, Blink came swooping round the corner – with Colonel Erick just behind him. When Erick saw the damage to the hangar – and to Teggs – his face filled with concern. "What happened here?"

Damona told him all that had gone on. "It's my fault, sir," she admitted. "I just couldn't wait to get inside."

"A good astrosaur never rushes into a situation blindly," Erick reminded her. "Blink was right to come to me for the key. Luckily, there's also a top-of-the-range robo-doctor stored on board that astro-jet." He hurried into the hangar and opened the doors. "It will treat your injuries, Teggs."

Moments later, Erick came back out with the robo-doctor – a silver cylinder on legs with a big red cross on the side. The robot crouched down beside Teggs and scanned his bruises with x-ray eyes.

"Front right and rear left limbs badly sprained," it said in a flat metallic voice.

"Beginning treatment." It flipped open its chest and squirted yellow gloop over Teggs.

"Spray-on bandages," Erick explained. "They come with built-in healing ointment."

"Will I be able to go on with the challenge?" Teggs asked hopefully.

"Negative," said the robo-doctor. "You must rest in bed. When you walk, you must use a crutch." The robot snapped off one of its metal legs and gave it to Teggs before promptly growing another one. "Here you go."

"Thanks," sighed Teggs.

"What about the instruments on the astro-jet?" asked Netta.

Damona looked at the flying instructor. "I'm sorry for what happened, of course . . . but can we use them to search for Admiral Rosso?"

Erick considered. "Only if your teams work together."

"But what about you, Teggs?" Blink squawked. "We can't leave you all alone."

43

"Of course you can!" Teggs insisted. "Working with the Darlings is your best chance of finding Rosso."

Dutch looked at Damona doubtfully. "I guess we could try."

"We're both a team-mate down," Damona said briskly. "Let's get on with it."

"All right," Blink sighed. "Take care, Teggs. See you soon."

Netta waved goodbye. "And if you find Splatt – tell him to sort himself out . . ."

Teggs watched the four cadets go into the sleek white-and-red astro-jet, followed by the robo-doctor. Then, leaning on his crutch, he managed to stand up.

Erick held out an arm. "I'll walk you to the dorm."

Teggs shook his head. "No need, sir. Please tell Commander Gruff I'm sorry I can't take part in the challenge."

"I'll tell him how you were injured, too," Erick assured him. "Now, rest up. We need you in good shape for Graduation Day – right?"

"Right," said Teggs. With a heavy heart and throbbing ankles, he hobbled back towards his room.

Damona was first inside the astro-jet and jumped straight into the pilot's seat. "Now, I know we're meant to share whatever's

on this ship," she said, "but I think one person needs to be in charge of everything, and that person should be me . . ."

Blink flew over her head and pecked the space radar's on-switch. "What did she say, Dutch?"

"I didn't hear a word." Dutch pushed past Damona, pulled a cable from the scanner screen and plugged it into the back of the radar. "There – now we can *all* see what's up in orbit."

Sure enough, a super-sharp view of space appeared on the screen, overlaid with a red radar grid that split it into eight sectors.

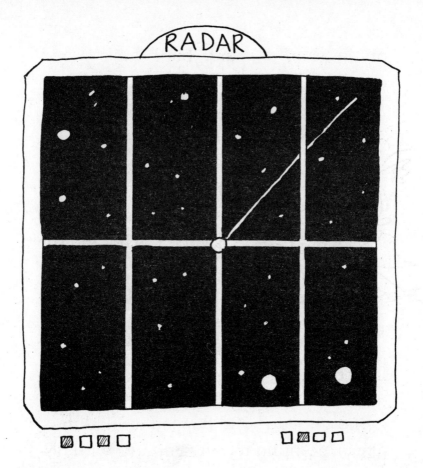

"I'll run a computer check on all objects in that area," said Netta, "so we know what's what."

"No need," said Dutch. "Blink's a big-time satellite spotter – he knows everything that's floating around up there."

Blink nodded and flapped around the screen, pointing to different dots with his beak. "That's a TV transmitter – that's a low-orbit fuel dump – that's a burned-out astro-carrier ..."

"Very impressive, geek-beak," said Damona. "But how about spotting something you *don't* recognize? That might be where they're holding Rosso!"

"Funny you should say that." Blink pointed to a blue blob. "This is solar station Zeta One. It predicts weather conditions around the planet. But guess what? It's not quite where it should be."

"Let's check." Netta pressed some buttons on the main computer. "You're right, Blink. It's off course by a quarter of a mile."

"Maybe something was trying to hide behind the solar station – and accidentally bumped it!" Eyes shining with excitement, Damona started twisting the flight controls, and the astro-jet's mighty engines rumbled into life.

"You're taking off," Dutch realized.

Blink sighed. "It doesn't feel right, going without Teggs."

"It stinks," Dutch agreed sadly, turning to Damona. "Especially since you and

Netta would be in hospital now if he hadn't saved you!"

"I feel bad about that," Damona admitted. "But think how rotten Teggs will feel if I don't make his sacrifice worth it by winning that medal!"

Blink rolled his eyes. "What about Splatt?"

"That's true," said Netta. "Shouldn't we wait in case he changes his mind about coming with us?"

"He told us to go," Damona pointed out. "Besides, there's no time to waste — we've got an admiral to save!"

Teggs had just reached the dino-dorms when he heard the *THROOM!* of engines. He couldn't help but smile as Erick's astro-jet zoomed low overhead, then climbed steeply into the sky. *That didn't take them long*, he thought. *Blink and Dutch will have Rosso rescued in no time!*

But then the doors in front of him

swung open, and two blue dino cleaners pushed past him with a trolley full of towels. One was tall and long-necked, the other was short and stumpy

Frowning, Teggs realized that they were the same two cleaners he'd seen talking to Splatt on Results Day. And with an even deeper frown he saw a familiar green arm poking out from the bottom of the trolley . . .

"Splatt!" Teggs cried. "What are you doing with Splatt?"

"We've been rumbled," rasped the short cleaner. "Run!"

Wincing with pain, Teggs chased after them in a wonky, two-legged gallop. The two dinos reached a nearby hover-speeder – part truck, part helicopter – threw open the rear doors and wheeled their trolley into the back. Gritting his teeth, Teggs used his crutch as a pole-vault to launch himself inside after them . . .

Only to find that the long-necked cleaner had a gun!

*ZZ-ZAPP!* Teggs yelped as a green ray-blast shocked through his bones. He collapsed in a heap and the doors slammed shut behind him.

The last thing he heard before the world went black was the creepy cleaners chuckling as they drove their prisoners away – to who knew where . . .

# Chapter Five

## MEETING THE ENEMY

High above the planet in their borrowed astro-jet, Dutch, Blink, Damona and Netta were getting close to their destination.

"Solar station Zeta One dead ahead," Damona reported. Sure enough, a large, spiky metal tangle was growing larger on the scanner screen.

"I don't see anything suspicious so far," said Netta.

"Wait!" Dutch hit the scanner's zoom switch. "What's that?"

Something dark was poking out from behind the weather station.

"Steer around Zeta One," said Blink

breathlessly. "Let's see!"

Damona edged the astro-jet past the solar station. A sinister black spaceship was parked behind it. It looked like a big ball, gleaming dimly in the starlight with stubby wings either side.

"That's got to be Rosso's hiding place," said Dutch as Damona pressed on the brakes. "Painted black to make it harder to spot in space."

Netta nodded. "And we've found him first!"

"We'd better move fast," said Blink. "The other cadets won't be far behind us."

"Maybe finding him was *too* easy," said Damona. "Rosso said there would be dangers to overcome."

Blink studied the dark unmarked spacecraft. "Perhaps we'll find them in there."

But even as he spoke, the astro-jet lurched forward.

"Whoa!" called Dutch. "Thought you said you could fly this crate?"

"I didn't press anything," Damona protested. "We're being pulled towards that black ship."

Blink gulped. "They must be using a space magnet!"

"We can't break free," cried Netta, struggling with the controls. "Whoever's on board that ship – they've got us!"

★

Back on Astro Prime, Teggs woke up
in darkness. His head hurt. His legs
throbbed. The floor beneath him was
gently trembling, and the *whoosh* of
an engine told him he was still in the
hover-speeder.

"Splatt?" he whispered.

"Teggs — is that you?" Splatt hissed back. "I'm tied up on this trolley."

"What's going on?" Teggs tried to get up, and gasped with pain — he'd been tied up too. "Who *are* those two dino cleaners? What are they up to?"

Splatt sighed. "The short one is Hex, the tall one's called Flippin. They hacked into the Academy's computers the night before Results Day and saw my low score. That's why they approached me. They said they could fix it so I got a better mark in my tests — provided I did something for them in return."

Teggs couldn't keep the dismay out of his voice. "You cheated?"

"I know it was wrong," Splatt moaned. "That's why I ran off before. You were so brave when you saved me and Damona and Netta — just like a *real* astrosaur. I couldn't be brave like that, no matter how much I cheated."

"Sometimes, admitting you're wrong can be the bravest thing of all," Teggs murmured.

Splatt sniffed sadly. "Anyway, I found the cleaners in the dino-dorms and asked them to change my score back to fifty-nine. Instead, they jumped me!"

"And got me too," Teggs grumbled. "What was it they made you do last night, anyway?"

"I had to disable a couple of security robots over on Saquaria, the Land of Wet Feet," Splatt explained. "It's lucky I'm fast – I had to whizz up and switch them off without being spotted."

"Saquaria's on the other side of the planet," Teggs realized. "No wonder you got so soggy last night. But where exactly *were* these robots?"

"Just outside the aqua-caves," said Splatt. "The robots stop anyone wandering in – but the cleaners really wanted to see those giant geysers, the Fountains of Fury."

"Did they now?" Teggs paused. "I wonder why . . ."

Suddenly, the hover-speeder's back doors were thrown open. Teggs gasped as the cleaners grabbed him and Splatt and hauled them out onto wet orange grass.

The speeder was parked behind a bush, and Teggs could just see two robotic sentries standing guard in front of a dripping-wet cave – ready to sound the alarm if anyone came or went. The booming roar of rushing water could be heard deep inside.

*We're a long way from the Academy,* Teggs thought grimly, *with no one we can call for help.*

Hex, the shorter cleaner, cut Splatt's ropes and passed him two small metal discs. "OK, Greenie – deal with those robots the same way you did last night."

Flippin, the taller cleaner, nodded. "If you don't, we'll shoot the stegosaurus with something nastier than a stun gun!"

Splatt sighed – and then shot off across the long grass like a scaly missile towards the nearest robot. Before it could turn – *WHAP!* Splatt slapped a disc on its side. The second robot swivelled round at the sound – but before it could spot Splatt, he had raced round behind it and stuck the other disc on its bottom.

To Teggs's surprise, both robots ignored Splatt as he ran back to the bush, and turned their attention on the cave again as if nothing had happened.

"Those discs reverse the security bots'

vision," Hex explained smugly, untying
the ropes around Teggs's legs. "For the
next thirty minutes they'll show the view
*behind* them – not in front."

Teggs scowled. "Meaning you can go
in and out of the cave without being
spotted."

"Yup." Flippin grinned nastily. "And we
can take prisoners with us too – so come
on. There's an old friend of yours who
can't wait to see you . . ."

Teggs hobbled across the grass and into
the cold, dark mouth of the cave. The

cleaners switched on torches to light up the darkness, pushing Teggs and Splatt along dank, dripping tunnels. The sound of rushing water grew louder. Teggs's heart began to pound as he saw murky light ahead. The tunnel widened into a round, shadowy cavern as big as a cathedral – and both cadets gasped at what they saw . . .

Gigantic jets of steaming hot water shot up with incredible force from a bubbling pool in the cavern's centre. And balanced on top of the super-spurting geysers – spluttering, and bobbing up and down in mid-air – was Admiral Rosso!

"I . . . I don't understand," Splatt stammered. "I thought Admiral Rosso was pretending to be kidnapped out in space?"

"Instead, he's been kidnapped for real," Teggs realized. "And while our friends are looking for him in space,

he's being kept out of sight down here."

"But rest assured your friends will find *something* waiting for them in orbit," came a sinister throaty voice. "And they will never be the same again."

Teggs peered around into the shadows. The voice sounded familiar. "Who's there?" he asked.

"I am!" A violet dinosaur with a sharp beaky mouth and long claws stepped out on her hind legs from behind a rock. "Remember me, Teggs? Commodore

Kallos – the Carnivore Crime Cartel's most evil agent." She smiled. "And I've got a plan that will rock the Dinosaur Space Service to its core!"

# Chapter Six

## KIDNAP CRISIS!

On board their stricken astro-jet, Dutch, Damona, Netta and Blink could only watch as the round black ship loomed ever larger on the scanner screen. A huge door slid silently open to reveal a launch bay. They were dragged inside, and an inner door closed behind them.

*CLANG!* The ship touched down and stayed there.

Netta checked the controls. "We're stuck. The space magnet is holding the

whole astro-jet to the floor."

Dutch nodded grimly. "Looks like we'll just have to go out and fight!"

The four excited cadets made their way to the main doors.

"There won't be any *real* bad guys," Blink reassured the others. "It's only a test."

"But no one ever won the Order of the Star Lizard for playing around," Damona reminded him. As they passed the robo-doctor, she smiled. "Luckily,

our mechanical medic can patch up
our opponents when we're through with
them!"

Dutch opened the astro-jet door, and
the cadets stepped out into the dark,
deserted launch bay. Along the far side
of the room they saw a line of doors.

"Which way do we go?" whispered
Netta.

Then, suddenly, light spilled out from
behind the door in the corner and a
hoarse voice called, "Help!"

"It's Rosso!" Damona exclaimed.

Dutch looked at Blink. "Do we dare to bust him out of here?" he asked.

"We dare!" Blink hissed back.

"Yeah, yeah, us too," said Netta impatiently. "Come on – sounds like he's in trouble!"

The four cadets rushed across the darkened chamber and charged through the open door, ready to face the enemy. But there was no one inside the metal room apart from the cadets themselves – and a digital recorder. "*Help!*" came the hoarse voice again from its little speakers.

"Rosso's not here at all," Blink squawked. "It's a trick!"

All at once, the door slammed shut behind them. "You mean a *trap*," groaned Dutch.

"Correct!" The scarred, scaly face of a carnotaur – a meat-eating dinosaur – pressed up against a small grille in the door. "Congratulations –  you're the first lot of cadets to fall for it. But you won't be the last." He chuckled, drool splashing from his jaws. "There are more astro-jets on their way here with your pals aboard. And we'll catch them as easily as we caught you!"

Damona glared at him. "Who are you?"

"I'm an agent of the Carnivore

Crime Cartel, horn-face," growled the carnotaur. "And from this moment on – you belong to us!"

Miles below, in the aqua-caves, Teggs gazed at Commodore Kallos in horror. "You," he breathed. "How did you get back to Astro Prime? I thought you were in space prison."

"I escaped with the help of my team and a handy dino-droid," Kallos revealed. "Then we hijacked a spaceship full of Academy cleaners coming back from holiday and took their places." She pointed to a huddle of dinosaurs tied up

in the shadows. "Getting past security was a cinch!"

"I suppose pretending to be cleaners is the perfect way to sneak about in plain sight," said Teggs. "Cleaners go everywhere."

"Even into Admiral Rosso's personal spacecraft." Flippin sniggered. "When the big greenie came on board last night, we were waiting."

Hex nodded proudly. "We squirted him with sleep gas and flew him here. His ship's parked deeper inside the caves, along with the cleaners' old crate."

"This disguise makes you quite tidy-minded," Flippin explained.

"But why leave poor Rosso bobbing up and down on those hot geysers?" said Teggs. "It's mean!"

"It's *necessary*," Kallos corrected him.

"Splooshed all about by the Fountains of Fury, he hasn't a hope of untying himself and coming to get us!"

"What do you want here, anyway?" Splatt demanded. "Last time, you tried to teach us cadets a load of rubbish so we'd make bad astrosaurs – and we beat you."

"But I'll have my revenge," Kallos rasped. "You and your friends will serve the carnivores well."

Teggs glared at her. "What are our friends facing up in space?"

"Rosso was planning to hide in an old space capsule full of training robots," said Hex, "but our space agents blew it to bits and hid their own ship in its place."

"As the cadets come on board in search of Rosso, they will be captured," Kallos gloated. "We shall take them all away to the Carnivore Sector for brainwashing – and you, Splatt and

Rosso too, of course. You will all be turned into secret meat-eater agents!"

"And then I suppose we'll 'escape' and come back to the DSS," Teggs concluded. "But really we'll be working for you – *against* the Vegetarian Sector."

"You will cause chaos and confusion at my command," Kallos agreed.

"And how will we get to this space-trap of yours?" Teggs enquired.

"We'll leave the same way we came," said Hex. "In the cleaners' spaceship."

Flippin nodded happily. "Plenty of room in there – and it smells really nicely of soap."

"I can't stand the thought of going to the Carnivore Sector."

Splatt fell whimpering in front of Kallos.

"Let me go, please! I'm not a top astrosaur, I'm a bottom astrosaur – or do I mean, a KNEE astrosaur?"

Kallos frowned. "Eh?"

Splatt suddenly shot between Kallos's knees, pushing past her and vanishing into the shadows. She squawked in alarm as she toppled over. Hex and Flippin ran to help her . . .

And Teggs struck!

He whacked Hex with his tail, and the carnivore cleaner went head over heels, squashing Flippin and Kallos as

he fell. Then, curling up into a spiky ball, Teggs catapulted himself over the startled meat-munchers. *I've got to get out of here*, he thought desperately, gasping as he bumped and rolled through rocky puddles. *Got to find help . . .*

"I don't care if those crummy cadets *are* on the Crime Cartel's most wanted list," screeched Kallos. "Forget the brainwashing – kill them!"

The next thing Teggs knew, there were laser bolts flying all around him, sizzling as

they struck water
and blasted
chunks out
of the walls.
He tumbled
behind a
boulder, his
two injured legs
throbbing with
pain, and looked
around desperately for any sign of Splatt.
But all he could see was Admiral Rosso
still poised precariously on the steaming
water-spouts.

"Sir!" Teggs yelled over the churning
roar of the geysers. Another laser beam
scorched past his head. "I'm stuck and
I can't find Splatt. Without your help,
we're finished!"

"Too right you are!" Kallos was back
on her feet and pulled a pistol from
her pocket. She fired it at the boulder –
which exploded!

The blast hurled Teggs into the
seething waters of the aqua-cave.
He spiralled helplessly through the inky
darkness of the underground spring,
tugged by a strong and merciless
current. *Got to reach the surface*,
he thought desperately.

But at the best of times it was
hard for a huge, heavy stegosaurus
like Teggs to swim, let alone with
two bad ankles. His lungs began
to ache. His head began to
spin. He turned his tail like
a propeller, trying to push
himself upwards. But
it was too difficult,
and the water was
growing scalding
hot, and he was
getting dizzier
with every
pounding
heartbeat . . .

*I can't make it*, he realized, sinking deeper into darkness. *The Carnivore Crime Cartel has won!*

## Chapter Seven

## TURNING THE TABLES

Just as Teggs's lungs were about to
explode, he felt something strong coil
itself around his body. *A sea serpent!* he
thought, struggling in its grip . . .

But suddenly, he found himself jerked
out of the dark depths and dangling
in dim daylight. Gasping for breath,
Teggs realized he was back at
the entrance to the aqua-
caves — and that the
"sea serpent"
was really the
long neck of
Commander
Gruff!

"Lucky I spotted you struggling in the stream, cadet," said Gruff. "The current was about to pull you deep underwater – never to be seen again."

"It's good to see *you* again, sir!" Teggs panted. "What are you doing here?"

"Academy computers don't make mistakes," the commander growled. "So when Splatt's score shot up, I smelled a rat and had him followed – by Sergeant Snoop, the undercover astrosaur."

A rugged blue dinosaur jumped out from behind Gruff's bulky body. "I saw

those phoney cleaners kidnap you both, Teggs," he explained. "So I threw a tracker onto their hover-speeder. As soon as the commander had got some troops together, we followed the signal here."

Gruff nodded. "And the sabotaged robots outside the aqua-cave showed us where you'd been taken."

"Those cleaners are working for Commodore Kallos," said Teggs breathlessly. "They've kidnapped Admiral Rosso too – he's hog-tied and helpless in the Fountains of Fury!"

"TIE ME UP, WOULD YOU?" A booming voice echoed down the tunnel. "Well, take THIS!"

"That's the admiral now," Gruff realized, as cries and clamour carried through the caves. He untwisted his neck, put Teggs down and called outside: "Troops – attack!"

Teggs watched as a six-strong squad of astrosaurs – led by a bright green

triceratops – charged past, following
Gruff and Snoop into the aqua-caves.
Wincing with pain, he hobbled after
them. "I'm not missing this for anything!"
he declared.

Eyes agleam, Teggs saw one sharp-
shooting astrosaur blast the gun from
Flippin's claws while another two
wrestled Hex to the ground as he tried

to escape. As for Kallos, she'd already been taken care of – by Admiral Rosso himself! He towered above everyone in the cavern, his giant, elephant-like foot pinning the commodore to the ground.

Teggs looked around anxiously, but there was no sign of Splatt.

"I'm glad to see you, Gruff," said Rosso calmly. "This evil traitor had me kidnapped – and her underlings are busy snaffling away your best cadets even as we speak!"

Gruff almost dropped his banana-cigar in shock.

"Luckily, one such cadet was here to untie me," Rosso went on – as a green figure peeped out from behind his neck.

"Splatt!" Teggs cried in relief. "I didn't know what had happened to you!"

"Sorry I seemed to vanish," said Splatt. "I knew Kallos would be out for my blood, so I jumped onto the big guy and hid till he could help!"

"No wonder I didn't see you," said Teggs. "You were very brave, leaping into the Fountains of Fury like that. But this is only half the rescue. Our friends are trapped on board Kallos's prison ship – we must get them out before they're brainwashed by carnivores!"

"Fat chance," wheezed Kallos from under Rosso's foot. "Our ship scans all approaching vessels with a special 'top cadet detector'. If it sees certain cadets are on 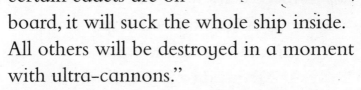 board, it will suck the whole ship inside. All others will be destroyed in a moment with ultra-cannons."

Sergeant Snoop scowled. "We'll send up our toughest warships."

But Gruff shook his head. "If we start a big space battle, the cadets could get hurt."

"My meat-eaters will crunch them and munch them up before you can save them," Kallos agreed.

"Commander Gruff, Admiral Rosso . . ." Teggs looked up at his superiors. "*I'm* one of the top cadets on the list. Kallos's computers will recognize me and let me on board. If I can just set my friends free, we can turn the tables on those carnivores,

I know it!"

Gruff shook his head. "No way, son."

"Look at the state of you, Teggs," said Snoop. "You're hardly fighting fit."

"But *I* am," said Splatt quietly. "My friends are up there too, and I want to help Teggs save them. Together, we'll stand a chance."

"Thanks, Splatt." Teggs turned to Gruff. "Commander, you can have a whole fleet of warships standing by to arrest those crummy kidnappers, but please – let us get on board first."

Gruff sighed. "What do you think, Admiral?"

"I think you've trained some of the finest dinosaurs in the whole Space Service," Rosso replied. "Dangerous as it is, I think this young stegosaurus's plan is our best hope to save the rest of your graduates."

"Agreed," said Snoop.

"Then I'll get you a ship, troops." Gruff

looked proudly down at Teggs and Splatt.
"I only wish I could get you a truckload
of good luck as well for what lies ahead
– you're going to need it!"

# Chapter Eight

## STORMING THE SHIP

Within the hour, Teggs and Splatt were blasting off in the last remaining astro-jet. All the others had been taken by cadets on the "space kidnap" challenge.

"Maybe not all our friends have been captured," said Splatt hopefully.

"No one has managed to get a warning message out to Gruff," Teggs reminded him, as Astro Prime's blue skies gave way to starry blackness. "We have to assume that all twenty-two of them have fallen into the carnivore trap."

Splatt sighed. "Which makes us their only hope of rescue."

Teggs thought of Dutch, Blink, Damona and Netta . . . of Trebor and the Baggy Brothers . . . of *all* his friends. "We won't fail you guys. We won't," he murmured.

"We'll soon be there," Splatt said nervously. "What are we going to do? *I* might be able to run, but you can hardly walk."

"I'll have to use my head instead of my legs." Teggs opened a storage locker and pulled out two white quilted outfits. "We'd better get changed into these."

"The emergency spacesuits?" Splatt
blinked. "Why?"

Teggs gave him a crooked smile.
"Because, believe me, we're about to
face the biggest emergency of our lives!"

On board the carnivore ship, Dutch and
Blink peered gloomily through the tiny
window in their cell door. The launch
bay beyond was now full of astro-jets.
Suddenly, a pale purple dinosaur with a
large headcrest appeared.

"Look!" said Dutch. "There's Lima the lambeosaur. She must have come here in that last ship."

Netta and Damona crowded forward. "Stay back!" they yelled to Lima.

Blink squawked his warning too. "It's a trap!"

"Get out of here!" Dutch hollered.

But Lima couldn't hear them. Like so many others before her, she suddenly took off towards a door in the wall, thinking Rosso was behind it – and was locked up the moment she was inside.

Dutch stamped his foot. "We haven't managed to save anyone."

"This really looks like the end," said Netta tearfully. "Teggs and Splatt will be graduating without us."

"It's not fair," moaned Damona. "Oh, *why* did we get ourselves caught like this? WHY?" She smashed her tail against the door with a colossal *KLANGG!* "OW! That really hurt."

Moments later, the cadets all gasped as a silver face pressed up against the cell window. "Hello," came a flat electronic voice. "Is anyone hurt?"

"It's the robo-doctor!" cried Netta.

Dutch stared. "But what's it doing here?" he asked.

"I am programmed to respond to any cry of pain," explained the robo-doctor. "If you are hurt, I must get into your cell and treat you."

Damona smiled at her friends. "Oh, I'm hurt all right!"

"And, er, I just bruised my wing!" said Blink quickly. "We both need treatment urgently."

Netta realized what they were doing and sat down heavily. "Oh, no! I just broke all my legs – and my tail and my neck too! Help!"

"Emergency treatment required," grated the robo-doctor. "Switching to mega-urgent cutting speed." Four saws unfolded from its body and started slicing

through the cell door with a screech of metal on metal.

Netta groaned. "That racket will bring every carnivore in the place running."

"They'll zap the robot and we'll be just as stuck as we were before," Dutch agreed.

"Hurry, robo-doctor," Blink pleaded, as the ear-splitting sawing went on. "You *must* hurry!"

"Look!" Splatt pointed at the astro-jet's scanner screen. "That must be the carnivore ship now."

Teggs narrowed his eyes at the sight
of the dark ball. Then the control room
shook as the jet suddenly lunged forward.
"They're pulling us in," he realized. "I
knew it – they must be using a space
magnet."

Splatt checked the controls. "We can't
break free," he said.

"We don't *want* to
break free." Teggs
pushed some
levers, and a
powerful hum
sounded through
the control room.
"If they really want
our ship, they can have it – with all
engines set to full power."

"We'll crash!" wailed Splatt.

"Why d'you think we're wearing
spacesuits?" Teggs reminded him. "Sit
down and I'll hit the ship's ejector
switch. Come on!"

Splatt hastily sat down
and Teggs whacked a
red button with his tail.
"EJECT!"

With a dizzying
*WHOOOSH!* both cadets
shot up through the emergency exit in
the roof. Teggs gulped. Stars and comets
seemed to spin and dance as he tumbled
through
space.
Then
the tiny
rockets
built
into his
backpack
fired and
brought
his crazy
course
under
control.

With Splatt floating beside him, he
watched as the astro-jet smashed into the
carnivore craft's launch bay like a giant
missile. There was a fantastic explosion
and the black ship tipped to one side,
smoke pouring from within.

"They weren't expecting that," Splatt
cried.

"But we're up against pros." Teggs

pulled a stun pistol from his pocket.
"It won't take them long to fight back."

Sure enough, carnivores in spacesuits
were already jetting out from their
damaged ship, weapons clutched in
their claws.

Teggs ducked as laser beams zipped
past his head. "Quickly, Splatt!" he
shouted, speeding through space and
returning fire. "We've got to get inside

before they can hurt our friends. It's time for the final face-off!"

★

Ba-*KOOOOM!* When the runaway astro-jet rammed into the launch bay, Dutch, Damona, Netta and Blink had been thrown to the floor. Alarms went off and red lights flashed.

"What was that?" Dutch cried.

The robo-doctor stopped sawing and its head spun in a circle. "Astrosaurs Academy jet J1L has just crashed into this vessel," it reported. "Scans show that no one was hurt. The jet was empty."

"Then whoever was on board escaped before it hit," Blink squawked. "It must be a rescue party!"

"We've got to get out and help them," Damona cried. "Robo-doctor, hurry!"

The robot started sawing again, attacking the door in a blaze of blue sparks until it had hacked out a good-sized hole. "There. Treatment can now begin."

Damona squeezed through the hole and patted the robot's head. "Thanks for getting us out. But we don't need a doctor any more."

"That's what *you* think," came a snarling hiss, as four towering carnotaurs in space armour stalked through the smoke. "Get back inside," said their leader, "or you'll be in hospital for a month."

"No way!" Dutch shouted.

Blink flew up into the air. "We've got to fight like never before!"

"And we don't dare fail," Netta added.

"ATTAAAAACK!" hooted Damona, as she charged the carnivores and battle commenced . . .

# Chapter Nine

## THE END OF THE BEGINNING

Outside the ship, Teggs and Splatt
whirled desperately through space,
dodging claws and lasers. A T. rex
loomed over Teggs, its space helmet
half full of drool. But Teggs smashed the
brute aside with his tail and fired a stun
blast up its bottom. With a high-pitched

squeal, it somersaulted away.

Splatt smashed a fierce raptor's rocket-pack with his gun and sent the snarling beast spiralling out of control. But more carnivores were flying out to join the fray.

"So tired," Splatt panted. "Can't keep going . . ."

"We must, Splatt!" Teggs urged him. "We *have* to reach our friends!"

Inside the ship, the escaped cadets were also fighting ferociously. Damona tore through the carnotaur ranks, horns flashing and big paws swiping. Dutch jumped from one baddie to another, squashing them to the deck. More meat-eaters rushed to the attack, but Netta met them with tooth-shattering tail strikes. Blink pecked at their ears and jabbed them in the eyes. While they flailed about in confusion, Damona head-butted their butts – while Dutch *butt*-butted their heads!

Then, suddenly, the launch bay's inner doors burst open – and a bunch of carnivores in spacesuits came flying in.

"Look out!" warned Netta as a raptor whizzed overhead.

Dutch caught a carnotaur in mid-air and smashed it to the floor. "Ha, these dudes go down easily."

"Too right," said Damona, flattening the suited T. rex which had fallen at her feet. "No challenge at all."

"And I think I know why." Blink flapped down to inspect the raptor, which had not moved since it landed. "Yes, just as I thought . . ."

"These carnivores were unconscious before they entered the ship," declared the robo-doctor. "Conclusion – they were actually *thrown* inside . . ."

"Correct!" Teggs and Splatt chorused, leaning wearily against each other in the launch-bay doorway.

"Guys!" cried Blink and Dutch.

"You found us!" cheered Damona
and Netta.

Staggering inside, their spacesuits
scratched and scuffed, Teggs and Splatt
fell into their friends' arms.

"We came here to save you," said
Splatt.

"But we should've known you'd have
the situation under control," Teggs added
with a grin. "You guys aren't cadets any

more – you're first-class astrosaurs!"

"And so are you two," Netta declared.

"That's for sure," Dutch agreed.

"Well, there's no time to waste," said Splatt. "We'd better contact Gruff and get a clean-up crew sent here."

"While you do that," said Teggs, "I'll start tying up these loser bruisers."

"We'll help," offered Dutch and Netta.

Damona turned to Blink. "Come on, beak-brain – let's start setting our friends free."

"Right-o, horn-head!" Blink jumped on the robo-doctor's back and steered it over to the nearest cell. "With our handy door-saw here, it shouldn't take too long."

"Good work, everyone." Teggs beamed round at his friends. "It looks as if we'll all be making Graduation Day tomorrow after all!"

Commander Gruff himself came to collect the cadets in a luxury transporter, while Sergeant Snoop took Kallos and her cronies away in a police ship – next stop: a super-secure space prison.

Teggs was so worn out he slept right through until dawn the next morning.

"Rise and shine, dude," Dutch called to his friend. "You can't miss Graduation Day!"

Blink beamed. "It's here at last!"

"We'll get our astrosaur uniforms," said Dutch.

"We'll get awards and certificates," Blink cooed.

"And we'll get to say goodbye," Teggs sighed. "You know, it'll be hard to leave. We've been a team for so long."

Dutch nodded. "We'll always be a team, dude."

"This isn't the end," Blink agreed. "It's just the end of the beginning. If either of you ever needed me, I'd be by your side in a flash."

"Same goes for me," Dutch declared.

"And me," said Teggs. "Always."

"Now, enough mush!" Dutch licked his lips. "Our leaving assembly doesn't start for another hour. I reckon we can fit in at least five breakfasts between now and then . . ." He held out his hand. "Do we dare?"

"One last time," Blink murmured, raising his wing.

Teggs placed his hand on theirs. "WE DARE!"

An hour later, with full tummies and broad smiles, Teggs, Dutch and Blink headed for the playing fields outside the Central Pyramid and took their places with the other graduating cadets. A huge crowd of friends and family had gathered to celebrate. Admiral Rosso was looking on proudly. The dinosaur press had sent reporters. Even top film director Stefano Spielsaur was there, recording the action for audiences across the Jurassic Quadrant.

Teggs felt a little dizzy with nerves. He saw that Damona and Netta were dolled up with extra-sparkly ribbons around their tails. Splatt was present too, jumping about with excitement.

"Isn't it great?" he cried. "Old Rosso put in a good word for me with Gruff. I'm allowed to graduate too."

"You put right what you did wrong," Teggs reminded him. "And after seeing you fight in space alongside me, I know you'll make a great astrosaur!"

"Well, I'll never cheat again," Splatt vowed. "That's for sure."

"But since Splatt's true score of fifty-nine still counts," said Damona, "the Daring Dinos are back as top team at Astrosaurs Academy." She smiled at Teggs, Blink and Dutch and held out her hand. "Oh, well. I *suppose* it's well deserved."

Teggs shook her hand. "Thank you, Damona."

"You and your darlings have made training a lot of fun," Blink added, shaking hands too.

Netta smiled at Dutch. "I suppose this is your proudest moment."

"Graduating, you mean?" the diplodocus asked.

"No," said Damona. "Shaking my hand!"

Dutch, Blink and Teggs groaned – but then Commander Gruff came on stage. The audience cheered and clapped.

"All right, everyone," boomed Gruff. "You're here to say congrats and so long to a very brave bunch of dinosaurs. They've trained hard and played hard . . . and now they've finally done it.

Today they will become astrosaurs!"

Teggs felt a swell of pride as the crowd burst into loud applause.

"But first things first," the commander went on. "May I welcome to the stage the most terrific team at this Academy . . . three brave boys who graduate today with honour – Teggs, Blink and Dutch, the Daring Dinos!"

As he stepped up to the stage with his best friends, Teggs could see two large

brown stegosaurus seated in the front row – his mum and dad, glowing with happiness. Gruff presented the three cadets with neatly folded red tops and wide black belts – the uniform of an astrosaur.

"And one extra-brave recruit has earned a very special privilege," Gruff went on. "Admiral Rosso will now present the Order of the Star Lizard – a medal awarded only five times in dinosaur history – to Teggs Horatio Stegosaur!"

The press reporters surged forward, camera flashes went off like a lightning storm, and the audience cheered and whistled and stamped their feet as Rosso hung an enormous gold medal round

Teggs's neck. The stegosaurus bowed.
Then he stretched the medal's ribbon as
wide as it would go so Blink and Dutch
could share his award. The crowd went
madder still! Even Damona's Darlings
did a victory dance.

Blink grinned. "I wonder what
adventures lie ahead?"

"We'll soon find out, dude." Dutch
smiled back. "Up there in outer space."

"But wherever we go and whatever we

find, we'll never forget the place that got us there." Teggs saluted Gruff and Rosso, then waved to the delighted audience. "Thanks for everything, Astrosaurs Academy. We'll be singing your praises to the stars – and beyond!"

# WHAT HAPPENED NEXT . . . ?

**Damona Furst** was made First Officer of the DSS *Herbivore*, the only pink spaceship in the fleet! She soon became its captain.

**Netta Arinetta** joined the DSS *Lizard Queen* as Security Officer, patrolling the Vegmeat Zone and keeping out carnivores.

**Linford Splatt** was made an officer in the Supply Fleet, delivering vital cargoes of food and equipment to dinosaurs in need.

**Dutch Delaney** became First Officer of the DSS *Starbloom*, enforcing the borders of the Vegetarian Sector and Sea Reptile Space.

**Blink Fingawing** was made Chief Navigator of *Deep Space Explorer One*, making maps of new stars and planets at the edge of the Jurassic Quadrant.

And **Teggs Stegosaur** was made Captain of the brand-new DSS *Sauropod* – finest ship in the Dinosaur Space Service – with immediate effect. Find out more by reading *Riddle of the Raptors* . . . and all the other *Astrosaurs* books!

# ALSO BY STEVE COLE

## MEET THE TIME - TRAVELLING COWS!

**COWS IN ACTION**

Genius cow Professor McMoo and his trusty sidekicks, Pat and Bo, are star gents of the C.I.A. – short for **COWS IN ACTION**! They travel through time, fighting evil bulls from the future and keeping history on the right track . . .

# IF YOU CAN'T TAKE THE SLIME
# DON'T DO THE CRIME!

Plog, Furp, Zill and Danjo aren't just monsters in a rubbish dump. They are crime-busting super-monsters, here to save their whiffy world!